D0526381

The Polka Palace Party
An Adventure in Teamwork

adapted by Erica David
based on the teleplay by McPaul Smith
illustrated by Warner McGee

SIMON AND SCHUSTER/NICKELODEON

Based on the TV series *Nick Jr. The Backyardigans*™ as seen on Nick Jr

SIMON AND SCHUSTER
First published in Great Britain in 2008 by Simon & Schuster UK Ltd
Africa House, 64-78 Kingsway, London WC2B 6AH

Originally published in the USA in 2006 by Simon Spotlight,
an imprint of Simon & Schuster Children's Division, New York.

A CIP catalogue record for this book is available from the British Library

ISBN 978-1-84738-220-7

Printed in China

10 9 8 7 6 5 4 3 2 1

Visit our websites: www.simonsays.co.uk www.nickjr.co.uk

Tyrone strolled out into the sunshine.
"Howdy," he said. "I'm Cowboy Tyrone,
and this here is my trusty tuba."
Tyrone blew into his tuba and played a polka tune.
"That's a mighty big sound," he said happily.

"I'm going to a surprise birthday party with my friend Sherman the Worman," explained Cowboy Tyrone. "The party is for Sherman's brother, and it's at the Polka Palace in Wyoming. I'm going to play my tuba so all the Wormans can dance the polka."

"We've got quite a ways to go to get to Wyoming," continued Cowboy Tyrone. "Come on, Sherman. Let's make tracks!"

Sherman the Worman and Cowboy Tyrone were moseying on their
way to the Polka Palace when they heard a voice call out for help.
It was a cowgirl, and she was in trouble!
"Hang on, pardner!" called Cowboy Tyrone.

Cowboy Tyrone ran to catch the cowgirl, who slipped from the branch and fell right into his tuba.

"Thanks, amigo!" the cowgirl exclaimed. "And thanks to your tuba, too!"

The cowgirl dusted herself off.

"Howdy!" she said. "I'm Cowgirl Uniqua. Now, where is my clarinet?"

"There it is," Cowboy Tyrone exclaimed.

"Thank goodness!" said Cowgirl Uniqua. "Without my clarinet, I couldn't play my favourite kind of music – the polka."

"The polka?" Cowboy Tyrone cried. "That's my favourite music too!"
Cowboy Tyrone invited Cowgirl Uniqua to come play polka music at
the Polka Palace.

Cowgirl Uniqua, Sherman the Worman, and Cowboy Tyrone made tracks across the great open plain.

Suddenly a group of horses thundered into their path. Then another cowboy came galloping after the horses.

"Help!" Cowboy Pablo shouted. "Runaway horses!"

"Don't worry," said Cowboy Tyrone. "If we all work together, we can stop them!"

Cowgirl Uniqua helped Cowboy Pablo open the gate to the corral.
Then Cowboy Tyrone blew into his tuba with all his might. To everyone's
amazement the horses stopped in their tracks and headed into the corral.

"Runaway horses always stop running when they hear a tuba,"
Cowboy Tyrone explained.

"Good thinking!" Cowgirl Uniqua said. "That was mighty fine
teamwork, pardners."

"Thanks, y'all," Cowboy Pablo said. "Now it's feeding time."

Cowboy Pablo picked up an accordion and played a
feeding-time song for the horses.

"That music sure sounds good," said Cowgirl Uniqua.
"It's my favourite kind of music – the polka," Cowboy Pablo replied.
Cowboy Tyrone and Sherman the Worman decided that Cowboy
Pablo should come play with them at the Polka Palace too.

At last the cowboys came to a mighty river.
"Look, a cowboy on a raft!" Cowboy Pablo said.

"Howdy," called Cowboy Tyrone. "We're going to a polka party. Could you give us a ride?"

"Sure, pardners," said Cowboy Austin.

"Say, are those your drums?" asked Cowgirl Uniqua.

"They sure are. I like to play the polka on them," Cowboy Austin replied.

"You play the polka too?" Cowboy Tyrone asked.
"You should come play at the Polka Palace with us," said Cowboy Pablo.
That gave Cowboy Tyrone an idea . . .

"Four instruments are better than one!" Cowboy Tyrone exclaimed.
"Together we could have a polka band."

"That's a great idea!" Cowgirl Uniqua cheered.
"Uh-oh, amigos. There's trouble ahead," Cowboy Pablo warned them.
They were heading right for a waterfall!

The cowboys worked together to lasso a tree branch.
Then they helped one another climb from the raft to safety—but
there wasn't time to save their instruments. The cowboys shook their
heads sadly as they watched the instruments plunge over the waterfall.

"Our instruments are gone, but I'm glad you're here, pardners,"
said Cowboy Pablo.

"We make a great team, amigos", Cowboy Tyrone agreed.
"And we can still make it to the Polka Palace for the party."

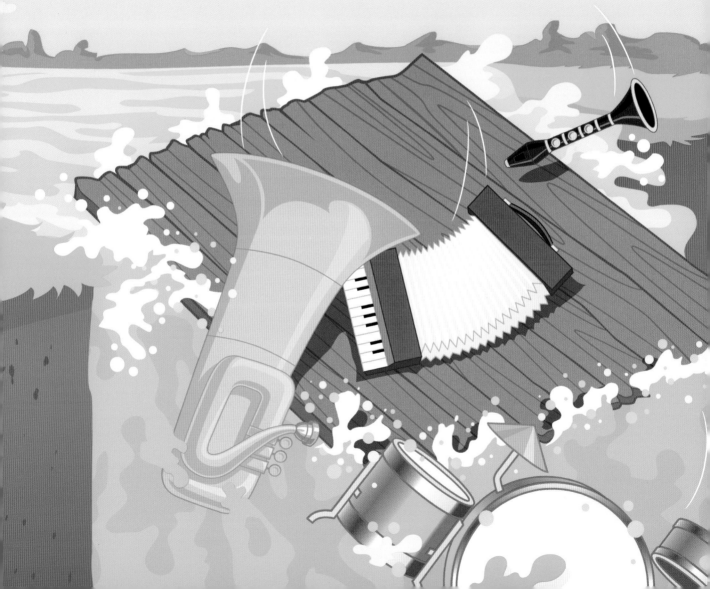

At the Polka Palace the cowboys found a surprise waiting for them.
"Our instruments!" Cowgirl Uniqua cried.
"The Wormans must have found them in the river and brought them here!" Cowboy Austin exclaimed. "Strong little fellers!"

Just then Sherman's brother arrived.

"Surprise!" yelled the polka band.

"I know just how to thank the Wormans for finding our instruments," said Cowboy Tyrone.

The cowboys picked up their instruments and began to play a polka song.

The Wormans danced and cheered.

When the song was finished, Cowboy Tyrone's tummy rumbled.
"I think it's time for a snack," he said.
"That's music to my ears," Cowgirl Uniqua agreed.
So the cowboys strolled on home for feeding time.